A THING THAT GLISTENED

(AND TWO OTHERS)

A THING THAT GLISTENED
(AND TWO OTHERS)

FRANK R. STOCKTON

WILDSIDE PRESS

A THING THAT GLISTENED AND TWO OTHERS

Published by Wildside Press LLC.

CONTENTS

A THING THAT GLISTENED 7

THE REVERSIBLE LANDSCAPE 16

PLAIN FISHING 31

A THING THAT GLISTENED

IN the fall of 1888 the steamship *Sunda*, from South-ampton, was running along the southern coast of Long Island, not many hours from port, when she was passed by one of the great British liners, outward bound. The tide was high, and the course of both vessels was nearer the coast than is usual — that of the *Sunda* being inside of the other.

As the two steamers passed each other there was a great waving of hats and handkerchiefs. Suddenly there was a scream from the *Sunda*. It came from Signora Rochita, the prima donna of an opera troupe, which was coming to America in that ship.

"I have lost my bracelet," she cried in Italian, and then, turning to the passengers, she repeated the cry in very good English.

The situation was instantly comprehended by every one. It was late in the afternoon; the captain had given a grand dinner to the passengers, at which the prima donna had appeared in all her glories of ornamentation, and the greatest of these glories, a magnificent diamond bracelet, was gone from the arm with which she had been enthusiastically waving her lace handkerchief.

The second officer, who was standing near, dashed into the captain's office and quickly reappeared with chart and instruments, and made rapid calculation of the position of the vessel at the time of the accident, making an allowance for the few minutes that had passed since the first cry of the signora. After consultation with the captain and recalculations of the distance from land and some other points, he announced to the weeping signora that her bracelet lay under a little black spot he had made on the chart, and that if she chose to send a diver for it she might get it, for the depth of water at that place was not great.

By profession I am a diver, and the next day I was engaged to search for the diamond bracelet of Signora Rochita. I had a copy of the chart, and, having hired a small schooner with several men who had been my assistants before, and taking with me all the necessary accouterments and appliances, I set out for the spot indicated, and by afternoon we were anchored, we believed, at or very near it. I lost no time in descending. I wore, of course, the usual diver's suit, but I took with me no tools nor any of the implements used by divers when examining wrecks, but carried in my right hand a brilliant electric lamp connected with a powerful battery on the schooner. I held this by an insulated handle, in which there were two little knobs, by which I could light or extinguish it.

The bottom was hard and smooth, and lighting my lamp I began to look about me. If I approached the bracelet I ought to be able to see it sparkle, but after wandering over considerable space, I saw no sparkles nor anything like a bracelet. Suddenly, however, I saw something which greatly interested me. It was a hole in the bottom of the ocean, almost circular, and at least ten feet in diameter. I was surprised that I had not noticed it before, for it lay not far from the stern of our vessel.

Standing near the rocky edge of the aperture, I held out my lamp and looked down. Not far below I saw the glimmer of what seemed to be the bottom of this subterranean well. I was seized with a desire to explore this great hole running down under the ordinary bottom of the sea. I signaled to be lowered, and although my comrades were much surprised at such an order, they obeyed, and down I went to the well. The sides of this seemed rocky and almost perpendicular, but after descending about fifteen feet they receded on every side, and I found myself going down into a wide cavern, the floor of which I touched in a very short time.

Holding up my lamp, and looking about me, I found myself in a sea cave, some thirty feet in diameter, with a dome-like roof, in which, a little to one side of the center, was the lower opening of the well. I became very much excited; this was just the sort of place into which a bracelet or anything else of value might be expected to have the bad luck to drop. I walked about and gazed everywhere, but I found nothing but rocks and water.

I was about to signal to be drawn up, when above me I saw what appeared to be a flash of darkness coming down through the well. With a rush and a swirl it entered the cavern, and in a moment I recognized the fact that a great fish was swooping around and about me. Its movements were so rapid and irregular, now circling along the outer edge of the floor of the cavern, then mounting above me, until its back seemed to scrape the roof, that I could not form a correct idea of the size of the creature. It seemed to me to be at least twenty feet along. I stood almost stupefied, keeping my eyes, as far as possible, fixed upon the swiftly moving monster.

Sometimes he came quite near me, when I shuddered in every fiber, and then he shot away, but ever gliding with powerful undulations of his body and tail, around, about, and above me. I did not dare to signal to be drawn up, for fear that the terrible creature would enter the well hole with me. Then he would probably touch me, perhaps crush me against the wall, but my mind was capable of forming no plans. I only hoped the fish would ascend and disappear by the way he came.

My mind was not in its strongest condition, being much upset by a great trouble, and I was so frightened that I really did not know what I ought to do, but I had sense enough left to feel sure that the fish had been attracted into the cavern by my lamp. Obviously, the right thing to do was to extinguish it, but the very thought of this nearly drove me into a frenzy. I could not endure to be left alone with the shark in darkness and water. It was an insane idea, but I felt that, whatever happened, I must keep my eyes upon him.

Now the great fish began to swoop nearer and nearer to me, and then, suddenly changing its tactics, it receded to the most distant wall of the cavern, where, with its head toward me, it remained, for the first time, motionless. But this did not continue long. Gently turning over on its side, it opened its great mouth, and in an instant, with a rush, it came directly at me. My light shone full into its vast mouth, glistening with teeth, and there was a violent jerk which nearly threw me from my feet, and all was blackness. The shark had swallowed my lamp! By rare good fortune, he did not take my hand also.

Now I frantically tugged at my signal rope. Without my lamp I had no thought but a desire to be pulled out of the water, no matter what happened. In a few minutes I sat, divested of my diving suit, and almost insensible, upon the deck of the schooner. As soon as I was able to talk I told my astonished comrades what had happened, and while we were discussing this strange occurrence, one of them, looking over the side, saw slowly rising to the surface the body of a dead shark.

"By George," he cried, "here is the beast. He has been killed by the current from the battery."

We all crowded to the rail and looked down upon the monster. He was about ten feet long, and it was plain that he had died for making himself the connection between the poles of the battery.

"Well," said the captain pleasantly. "I suppose you are not going down again?"

"Not I," I replied. "I give up this job."

Then suddenly I cried:

"Come boys, all of you. Make fast to that shark, and get him on board. I want him."

Some of the men laughed, but my manner was so earnest that in a moment they all set about to help me. A small boat was lowered, lines were made fast to the dead fish with block and tackle, and we hauled him on deck. I then got a butcher's knife from the cabin and began to cut him open.

"Look here, Tom!" exclaimed the captain, "that's nonsense. Your lamp's all smashed to pieces, and if you get it out, it will never be any good to you."

"I don't care for the lamp," I answered, working away energetically, "but an idea has struck me. It's plain that this creature had a fancy for shining things. If he swallowed a lamp, there is no reason why he should not have swallowed anything else that glittered."

"Oho!" cried the captain, "you think he swallowed the bracelet, do you?"

And instantly everybody crowded more closely about me.

I got out the lamp. Its wires were severed as smoothly as if they had been cut by shears. Then I worked on. Suddenly there was a cry from every man. Something glimmered in the dark interior of the fish. I grasped it and drew it out. It was not a bracelet, but a pint bottle which glimmered like a glow-worm. With the bottle in my hand, I sat upon the deck and gazed at it. I shook it. It shone brighter. A bit of oiled silk was tied tightly over the cork, and it was plain to see that it was partly filled with a light colored oil, into which a bit of phosphorous had been dropped, which, on being agitated, filled the bottle with a dim light.

But there was something more in the bottle than phosphorus and oil. I could see a tin tube, corked at each end, and the exposed parts of the corks spreading enough to prevent the tin from striking the glass.

We all knew that this was one of those bottles containing a communication of some sort, which are often thrown into the sea, and float about until they are picked up. The addition of the oil and phosphorus was intended to make it visible by night as well as by day, and this was plainly the reason why it had been swallowed by a light-loving shark.

I poured out the oil and extracted the tube. Wiping it carefully, I drew out the corks, and then, from the little tin cylinder, I pulled a half sheet of note paper, rolled up tightly. I unrolled it, and read these words:

Before I jump overboard, I want to let people know that I killed John Polhemus. So I have fixed up this bottle. I hope it may be picked up in time to keep Jim Barker from being hung. I did think of leaving it on the steamer, but I might change my mind about jumping overboard, and I guess this is the best way. The clothes I wore and the hatchet I did it with are under the woodshed, back of Polhemus's house.

Henry Ramsey.

I sprang to my feet with a yell. Jim Barker was my brother, now lying in prison under sentence of death for the murder of Polhemus; all the circumstantial evidence, and there was no other, had been against him. The note was dated eight months back. Oh! cruel fool of a murderer.

The shark was thrown overboard, and we made best speed to port, and before the end of the afternoon I had put Ramsey's note into the hands of the lawyer who had charge of my brother's case.

Fortunately he was able to identify the handwriting and signature of Ramsey, a man who had been suspected of the crime, but against whom no evidence could be found. The lawyer was almost as excited as I was by the contents of this note, and early the next morning we started together for the house of the Polhemus family. There, under the woodshed, we found carefully buried a bloodstained shirt and vest, and the hatchet.

My impulse was to fly to my brother, but this my lawyer forbade. He would take charge of the affair, and no false hopes must be excited, but he confidently assured me that my brother was as good as free.

Returning to the city, I thought I might as well make my report to Signora Rochita. The lady was at home and saw me. She showed the most intense interest in what I told her, and insisted upon every detail of my experiences. As I spoke of the shark, and the subterranean cave, she nearly fainted from excitement, and her maid had to bring her smelling salts. When I had finished, she looked at me steadily for a moment, and then said:

"I have something to tell you, but I hardly know how to say it. I never lost my bracelet. I intended to wear it at the captain's dinner, but when I went to put it on I found the clasp was broken, and, as I was late, I hurried to the table without the bracelet, and thought of it no more until, when we were all waving and cheering, I glanced at my wrist and found it was not there. Then, utterly forgetting that I had not put it on, I thought it had gone into the sea. It was only this morning that, opening what I supposed was the empty box, I saw it. Here it is."

I never saw such gorgeous jewels.

"Madame," said I, "I am glad you thought you lost it, for I have gained something better than all these."

"You are a good man," said she, and then she paid me liberally for my services. When this business had been finished, she asked:

"Are you married?" I answered that I was not.

"Is there any one you intend to marry?"

"Yes," said I.

"What is her name?" she asked.

"Sarah Jane McElroy."

"Wait a minute," said she, and she retired into another room. Presently she returned and handed me a little box.

"Give this to your ladylove," said she; "when she looks at it, she will never forget that you are a brave man."

When Sarah Jane opened the box, there was a little pin with a diamond head, and she gave a scream of delight. But I saw no reason for jumping or crying out, for after having seen the Signora's bracelet, this stone seemed like a pea in a bushel of potatoes.

"I don't need anything," she said, "to remind me that you are a brave man. I am going to buy furniture with it."

I laughed, and remarked that "every little helps."

When I sit, with my wife by my side, before the fire in our comfortable home, and consider that the parlor carpet, and the furniture and the pictures, and the hall and stair carpet, and all the dining-room furniture, with the china and the glass and the linen, and all the kitchen utensils, and two bedroom suits on the second story, both hardwood, and all the furniture and fittings of a very pleasant room for a single man, the third story front, were bought with the pin that the signora gave to Sarah Jane, I am filled with profound respect for things that glitter. And when I look on the other side of the fire and see Jim smoking his pipe just as happy as anybody, then I say to myself that, if there are people who think that this story is too much out of the common, I wish they would step in here and talk to Jim about it. There is a fire in his eyes when he tells you how glad he is that it was the shark instead of him, that is very convincing.

THE REVERSIBLE
LANDSCAPE

TO LOOK at me no one would suppose it; but it is, nevertheless, a fact that I am a member of a fire company. I am somewhat middle-aged, somewhat stout, and, at certain times of the year, somewhat stiff in the joints; and my general dress and demeanor, that of a sober business man, would not at all suggest the active and impetuous fireman of the period. I do not belong to any paid department, but to a volunteer Hook and Ladder Company, composed of the active-bodied or active-minded male citizens of the country town where I live. I am included in the active-minded portion of the company; and in an organization like ours, which is not only intended to assist in putting out the fires of burning buildings, but to light the torch of the mind, this sort of member is very valuable. In the building which we occupy, our truck, with its hooks and ladders, stands upon the lower floor, while the large room above is used as a club and reading-room. At the beginning of the first winter of our occupancy of the building, we found that this room, which had been very pleasant in summer, was extremely uncomfortable in winter. The long apartment had been originally intended for purposes of storage; and although we had ornamented it and fitted it up very neatly, a good deal of carpentry and some mason's work was necessary before it could be made tight and draught-proof for cold weather. But lately we had spent money very freely, and our treasury was absolutely empty. I was chairman of the committee which had charge of everything pertaining to our rooms, and I felt the responsibilities of my position. The necessary work should be begun immediately, but how could the money be raised to pay for it? Subscriptions for this and that had been made until the members were tired of that sort of thing; and the ill success of the last one showed that it would not do to try it again.

I revolved in my mind a great many plans for raising the sum required, and one morning, as I was going to my place of business in the city, I was seized with a happy idea. At the moment of seizure I was standing in front of a large show-window, in which were a number of oil paintings, all of them very fresh and bright. "How would it do," thought I to myself, "to buy a picture at a moderate price and put it up at a raffle? People who are not willing to give money outright will often enter into a scheme of this kind. I will go in and make inquiries."

When I entered I found myself in a large showroom, the walls of which were covered with paintings. A person advanced to meet me who, as it soon became evident, was the proprietor of the place. He was a large man, dressed in black, with an open shirt-front and an expansive countenance. His eyes and hair were black, and his ears stood out from his head in a manner which, according to a recent writer, indicates the money-getting faculty; and he plainly belonged to that class of persons who in the Middle Ages did not, as is the present custom, pay money for having their teeth extracted, but often disbursed large sums for the privilege of retaining them. When I asked him if I could procure a good and effective picture at a moderate price, he threw out his chest and waved his arms toward his walls. "There, sir," he said, "you can see oil paintings of every subject, of every style, and of every class; and at prices, sir, lower than they can be found elsewhere in the known world. Mention the kind of picture you want, and I can accommodate you."

I replied that I did not know exactly what I wanted, and that I would see what he had. I now began to look at the pictures on the walls, occasionally mentioning my ideas in regard to their merits, when suddenly my companion turned to me and said:

"Are you connected with the press, sir?"

I replied that I was not, although I occasionally wrote for periodicals.

"Upon art subjects?" he asked.

I answered in the negative.

"Then you are unprejudiced," he said, "and I believe from your appearance that you are a man of influence, and there is nothing I would like better than to exhibit the workings of my art organization to a man of influence, unprejudiced on the subject. My object is, sir, to popularize art; to place high art within the reach of the masses, and thus to educate the artistic faculties of even the poorest citizens."

I said that I supposed the chromo movement was intended to do all that.

"No, sir," he replied, warmly; "chromos cannot accomplish the object. They are too expensive; and, besides, they are not the real thing. They are printed, not painted; and what the public wants is the real thing, the work of the brush; and that is what I give them. The pictures you see here, and an immense stock besides, are all copies of valuable paintings, many of them in the finest galleries of Europe. I sell no originals. I guarantee everything to be a copy. Honesty is at the bottom of all I do. But my copies are exactly like the originals; that is all I claim. I would like, sir, to show you through my establishment, and let you see how I am carrying on the great work of art education. There are picture-dealers in this city, sir, plenty of them, who try to make the public believe that the vile daubs they sell are originals, and the works of well-known painters; and when they do admit that the picture is a copy, they say it is the work of some distinguished student; that there is no other copy in the country; or they make some other misstatement about it. These people conceal their processes, but their tricks are beginning to be well known to the public. Now, sir, I conceal nothing. The day for that sort of thing is past. I want men of influence to know the facilities I have for the production of art-work upon a grand scale. We will first go into the basement. Sir," said he, as I followed him downstairs, "you know how the watch-making business has been revolutionized by the great companies which manufacture watches by machinery. The slow, uncertain, and expensive work of the poor toilers who made watches by hand has been superseded by the swift, unerring, and beautiful operations of machinery and steam. Now, sir, the great purpose of my life is to introduce machinery into art, and, ultimately, steam. And yet I will have no shams, no chromos. Everything shall be real—the work of the brush. Here, sir," he continued, showing me into a long room filled with workmen, "you see the men engaged in putting together the frames on which to stretch my canvases. Every stick is cut, planed, and jointed at a mill in Vermont, and sent on here by the car-load. Beyond are the workmen cutting up, stretching, and preparing the canvas, bales upon bales of which are used in a day. At the far end are the mills for grinding and mixing colors. And now we will go to the upper floors, and see the true art-work. Here, sir," he said, continuing to talk as we walked through the rooms on the various floors, "is the landscape and marine department. That row of men are putting in skies; they do nothing else. Each has his copy before him, and, day after day, month after month, paints nothing but that sky; and of course he does it with great rapidity and fidelity. Above, on those shelves, are sky-pots of every variety; blue-serene pots, tempest pots, sunset pots in compartments, morning-gray pots, and many others. Then the work passes to the middle-ground painters, who have their half-tone pots within easy reach. After that the foreground men take it up, and the figurists put in the men and animals. That man there has been painting that foreground cow ever since the first of August. He can now put her in three and a half times in fifteen minutes, and will probably rise to sixteen cows an hour by the end of this month. These girls do nothing but put white-caps to waves. There's a great demand at present for the windy marine. This next room is devoted to portraits to order. You see that row of old ladies without heads, each holding a pair of spectacles, and with one finger in the Bible to keep the place; that's very popular, and we put in a head when the photograph is sent. There is a great rage at present for portraits of babies without any clothes on. Here is a lot of undraped infants with bodies all finished, but with no heads. We can finish them to order at very short notice. I have one girl who puts in all the dimples. You would be surprised to see what a charming dimple she can make with one twist of her brush. Long practice at one thing, sir, is the foundation of the success of this great establishment. Take that girl away from her dimple-pot, and she is nothing. She is now upstairs, putting dimples into a large Correggio order from the West. This next room is our figure department, battle-pieces, groups, single figures, everything. As you have seen before, each man only copies from the original that part which is his specialty. In addition to its other advantages, this system is a great protection to us. None of my men can work at home at nights and Sundays, and forge pictures. Not one of them can do a whole one. And now, sir, you have seen the greater part of my establishment. The varnishing, packing, and storage rooms are in another building. I am now perfecting plans for the erection of an immense edifice with steam-engines in the cellar, in which my paintings shall be done by machinery. No chromos, mind you, but real oil-paintings, done by brushes revolving on cylinders. I shall have rolls of canvas a mile long, like the paper on which our great dailies are printed, and the machines shall do everything; cut off the picture, when it has passed among the cylinders, whereupon fresh canvas will be rolled in for a new one; another machine will stretch them; and they will pass through a varnish bath in the twinkling of an eye. But this is in the future. What I want of you, sir, and of other men of influence in society, is to let our people know of the great good that is ready for them now, and of the greater benefit that is coming. And, more than that, you can do incalculable good to our artists. Those poor toilers on the solitary canvas should know how to become prosperous, great, and happy; tell them to go into some other business. And now, sir, I must see what I can do for you. We will return to my gallery, and I will show you exactly what you want."

When we reached the back part of the showroom, down-stairs, he brought out an unframed picture about three feet long and two high, and placed it in a favorable light. "There," said he, "is a picture which will suit you. It is what we call a reversible landscape, and is copied from the only genuine picture of the kind in the world. It is just as good as two pictures. In this position, you see, a line of land stretches across the middle of the picture, with trees, houses, and figures, with a light sky above and a lake, darker in hue, below. Everything on the land is reflected accurately in the water. It is a landscape in morning light. Turn it upside down, so, and it is an evening scene; darkening sky above, light water beneath; the morning star, which you saw faintly glimmering in the other picture, is now the reflection of the evening star."

I do not pretend to be a judge of pictures, but I fancy I appreciate an original idea when I see it, and I thought that this picture might answer my purpose. "What is the price of the painting?" I asked.

"Well, sir," said he, "to you, as a man of influence, I will fix the price of this great painting, from a comparatively unknown work of Gaspar Poussin, at four dollars and a half."

In spite of what I had seen of the facilities possessed by this establishment for producing cheap work, I must confess that I was surprised at the smallness of the sum asked for an oil-painting of that size; I had expected to give forty or fifty dollars. But, although I am not a judge of paintings, I am a business man, and accustomed to make bargains. Therefore I said:

"I will give you two dollars and fifty cents for the picture."

"Done," said he. "Where shall I send it?"

I gave him my city address, and paid the money. As he accompanied me to the door, he said: "If you would like more of these pictures, I will sell you one dozen for eighteen dollars, or the whole lot of one hundred, just finished—and there will be no more of them painted—for one hundred dollars." I told him one was all I wanted, and departed. I carried the picture home that afternoon, and in the evening exhibited it at our club-room, and made known my scheme for raising the money we needed by getting up a raffle with this painting as the prize; one hundred tickets at the low price of two dollars each. The reversible landscape was set up, first one way and then the other, a great many times, and created quite a sensation.

"I don't think it's worth the half of two hundred dollars," said Mr. Buckby, our president, "but as the money is for the use of our Association, I don't mind that. But my objection to the scheme is that, if I should gain the prize, I should be laughed at by all my fellow-members: for, to tell the truth, I think that painting is a good deal more funny than otherwise. It's not what I call high art."

The other members generally agreed with him. They were very much amused by the picture, but they did not care to possess it, imagining that those who ridiculed it might also ridicule its owner. This opposition discouraged me, and I retired to reflect. In about five minutes I returned to the company, which had now greatly increased, as it was one of our regular meeting nights, and I asked if they would consent to this raffle if I would engage that the winner of the picture should not be laughed at by any other member.

"How will you guarantee that?" asked Mr. Buckby.

"I will put the matter in the hands of the Association," I answered. "If, after the raffle is over, a majority of the members shall decide that any of us have reason to laugh at the winner of this painting, I will refund all the money paid for tickets."

There was something in this proposition which aroused the curiosity of my fellow-firemen; and when the meeting was called to order, a resolution was adopted that we would have the raffle, and that the management of it should be placed in my hands, subject to the conditions mentioned above. There were a good many surmises as to what I was going to do to keep the people from laughing at the prize-winner, the general opinion being that I intended to have the picture altered so that it would be like an ordinary landscape, and not reversible. But the affair was something novel, and promised to put the much-needed money into our treasury; and several gentlemen assured me that they would make it their business to see that every member took a ticket, one generous man promising, in the interests of the Association, to present them to such of the few members as might decline to buy them for themselves. This offer was made in consequence of my insistance that every one of us should have a chance in the raffle.

The next morning I went to the art-factory and told the proprietor that I would take the lot of reversibles he had on hand, if he would include the one already purchased, and receive ninety-seven dollars and a half as the balance due.

"All right!" said he. "I have the ninety-nine still on hand. Are you in the tea business, sir?"

"Oh, no," said I; "the pictures are intended for a large Association."

"No better way of extending the influence of art, sir," he said, heartily. "I shall charge you nothing for boxing. The same address, sir?"

"No, they must be forwarded to my residence," and I gave him the needful directions, and a check.

The next day the ninety-nine pictures arrived and were stored in my barn. My wife, to whom I had told my plan, made some objections to it, saying it did not seem right to use half the money paid in to buy so many pictures; but I told her that no one could expect in a raffle to clear all the money subscribed, and that although we should not gain as much as I had hoped, we should clear a hundred dollars, and every man would have a picture. This was surely fair, and the fact was that the unsympathetic state of mind of our members made it necessary for me to do something of this kind, if I expected to raise the needed money at all.

The raffle was announced, and on the appointed evening there was a full attendance. The prize was won by a Mr. Horter, an art-collector of a nervous temperament, who had objected to the raffle, and who had consented to buy a ticket only after repeated solicitations.

"Now mind," he said to me, "you promised that the other men should not laugh at me, and I hold you to your contract."

I answered that I intended to stand by it, and that the painting should be sent to him in the morning from my house, whither it had been removed. Every member present announced his intention of calling on Horter the following evening to see why he should not be laughed at.

All the next forenoon my man, with a horse and light wagon, was engaged in delivering the reversible landscapes, one to every member of our club. These gentlemen were, in almost every case, absent at their places of business. When they came home in the evening each found his picture, with his name on the back of it, and a printed slip informing him that in this raffle there had been no blanks, and that every man had drawn a prize.

Not a man called upon Mr. Horter that evening, and he greatly wondered why they did not come in, either to laugh or to say why they should not do so; but every other member of our club was visited by nearly all his fellow-firemen, who ran in to see if it were true that he also had one of those ridiculous reversible landscapes. As everybody knew that Mr. Horter had one, there was no need to call on him; and even if they had hoped to be able to laugh at him they could not do so, when each of them had drawn one of the pictures himself. A good many called on me, and some were a little severe in their remarks, saying that although it might be a very pretty joke, I must have used up nearly all the money that they had given for the good of the Association, for, of course, none of them cared for the absurd prize.

But when, on the next meeting night, I paid in one hundred dollars to the treasury, a sum more than sufficient to make our room comfortable, they were quite satisfied. The only thing that troubled them was to know what to do with the pictures they had drawn. Not one of them was willing to keep his pre-posterous landscape in his house. It was Mrs. Buck-by, our president's wife, who suggested a way out of the difficulty.

"Of course," she said to her husband, "it would have been much better if each one of you had given the two dollars without any raffle, and then you would have had all your money. But one can't expect men to do a thing like that."

"Not after we had all paid in our regular dues, and had been subscribing and subscribing for this, that, and the other thing for nearly a year," said I, who was present at the time. "Some extra inducement was necessary."

"But, as you have all those horrid landscapes," she continued, "why don't you take them and put them up along the top of your walls, next the ceiling, where those openings are which used to ventilate the room when it was used for storage? That would save all the money that you would have to pay to carpenters and painters to have those places made tight and decent-looking; and it would give your room a gorgeous appearance."

This idea was hailed with delight. Every man brought his picture to the hall, and we nailed the whole hundred in a row along the top of the four walls, turning one with the darker half up, and the next the other way, so as to present alternate views of morning and evening along the whole distance. The arrangement answered admirably. The draughts of air from outside were perfectly excluded: and as our walls were very lofty, the general effect was good.

"Art of that kind cannot be too high," said Mr. Horter.

A week or two after this, when I arrived at home one afternoon, my wife told me that there was a present for me in the dining-room. As such things were not common, I hurried in to see what it was. I found a very large flat package, tied up in brown paper, and on it a card with my name and a long inscription. The latter was to the effect that my associates of the Hook and Ladder Company, desirous of testifying their gratitude to the originator and promoter of the raffle scheme, took pleasure in presenting him with the accompanying work of art, which, when hung upon the walls of his house, would be a perpetual reminder to him of the great and good work he had done for the Association.

I cannot deny that this pleased me much.

"Well!" I exclaimed to my wife, "it is very seldom that a man gets any thanks for his gratuitous efforts in behalf of his fellow-beings; and although I must say that my services in raising money for the Association deserved recognition, I did not expect that the members would do themselves the justice to make me a present."

Unwrapping the package, I discovered, to my intense disgust, a copy of the Reversible Landscape! My first thought was that some of the members, for a joke, had taken down one of the paintings from our meeting-room and had sent it to me; but, on carefully examining the canvas and frame, I was quite certain that this picture had never been nailed to a wall. It was evidently a new and fresh copy of the painting of which I had been assured no more would be produced. I must admit that I had felt a certain pride in decorating our hall with the style of picture that could not be seen elsewhere; and, moreover, I greatly dislike to be overreached in business matters, and my wrath against the manufacturer of high art entirely overpowered and dissipated any little resentment I might have felt against my waggish fellow-members who had sent me the painting.

Early the next morning I went direct to the art-factory, and was just about entering when my attention was attracted by a prominent picture in the window. I stepped back to look at it. It was our reversible landscape, mounted upon an easel, and labelled "A Morning Scene." While I examined it to assure myself that it was really the landscape with which I was so familiar, it was turned upside down by some concealed machinery, and appeared labelled, "An Evening Scene." At the foot of the easel I now noticed a placard inscribed: "The Reversible Landscape: A New Idea in Art."

I stood for a moment astounded. The rascally picture-monger had not only made another of these pictures, but he was prepared to furnish them in any number. Rushing into the gallery, I demanded to see the proprietor.

"Look here!" said I, "what docs this mean? You told me that there were to be no more of those pictures painted; that I was to possess a unique lot."

"That's not the same picture, sir," he exclaimed. "I am surprised that you should think so. Step outside with me, sir, and I'll prove it to you. There, sir!" said he, as we stood before the painting, which was now Morning side up, "you see that star? In the pictures we sold you the morning star was Venus; in this one it is Jupiter. This is not the same picture. Do you imagine that we would deceive a customer? That, sir, is a thing we never do!"

PLAIN FISHING

"WELL, SIR," said old Peter, as he came out on the porch with his pipe, "so you came here to go fishin'?"

Peter Gruse was the owner of the farm-house where I had arrived that day, just before supper-time. He was a short, strong-built old man, with a pair of pretty daughters, and little gold rings in his ears. Two things distinguished him from the farmers in the country round about: one was the rings in his ears, and the other was the large and comfortable house in which he kept his pretty daughters. The other farmers in that region had fine large barns for their cattle and horses, but very poor houses for their daughters. Old Peter's ear-rings were indirectly connected with his house. He had not always lived among those mountains. He had been on the sea, where his ears were decorated, and he had travelled a good deal on land, where he had ornamented his mind with many ideas which were not in general use in the part of his State in which he was born. His house stood a little back from the high road, and if a traveller wished to be entertained, Peter was generally willing to take him in, provided he had left his wife and family at home. The old man himself had no objection to wives and children, but his two pretty daughters had.

These young women had waited on their father and myself at supper-time, one continually bringing hot griddle cakes, and the other giving me every opportunity to test the relative merits of the seven different kinds of preserved fruit which, in little glass plates, covered the otherwise unoccupied spaces on the tablecloth. The latter, when she found that there was no further possible way of serving us, presumed to sit down at the corner of the table and begin her supper. But in spite of this apparent humility, which was only a custom of the country, there was that in the general air of the pretty daughters which left no doubt in the mind of the intelligent observer that they stood at the wheel in that house. There was a son of fourteen, who sat at table with us, but he did not appear to count as a member of the family.

"Yes," I answered, "I understood that there was good fishing hereabout, and, at any rate, I should like to spend a few days among these hills and mountains."

"Well," said Peter, "there's trout in some of our streams, though not as many as there used to be, and there's hills a plenty, and mountains too, if you choose to walk fur enough. They're a good deal furder off than they look. What did you bring with you to fish with?"

"Nothing at all," I answered. "I was told in the town that you were a great fisherman, and that you could let me have all the tackle I would need."

"Upon my word," said old Peter, resting his pipe-hand on his knee and looking steadfastly at me, "you're the queerest fisherman I've see'd yet. Nigh every year, some two or three of 'em stop here in the fishin' season, and there was never a man who didn't bring his jinted pole, and his reels, and his lines, and his hooks, and his dry-goods flies, and his whiskey-flask with a long strap to it. Now, if you want all these things, I haven't got 'em."

"Whatever you use yourself will suit me," I answered.

"All right, then," said he. "I'll do the best I can for you in the mornin'. But it's plain enough to me that you're not a game fisherman, or you wouldn't come here without your tools."

To this remark I made answer to the effect that, though I was very fond of fishing, my pleasure in it did not depend upon the possession of all the appliances of professional sport.

"Perhaps you think," said the old man, "from the way I spoke, that I don't believe them fellers with the jinted poles can ketch fish, but that ain't so. That old story about the little boy with the pin-hook who ketched all the fish, while the gentleman with the modern improvements, who stood alongside of him, kep' throwin' out his beautiful flies and never got nothin', is a pure lie. The fancy chaps, who must have ev'rythin' jist so, gen'rally gits fish. But for all that, I don't like their way of fishin', and I take no stock in it myself. I've been fishin', on and off, ever since I was a little boy, and I've caught nigh every kind there is, from the big jew-fish and cavalyoes down South, to the trout and minnies round about here. But when I ketch a fish, the first thing I do is to try to git him on the hook, and the next thing is to git him out of the water jist as soon as I kin. I don't put in no time worryin' him. There's only two animals in the world that likes to worry smaller creeturs a good while afore they kill 'em; one is the cat, and the other is what they call the game fisherman. This kind of a feller never goes after no fish that don't mind being ketched. He goes fur them kinds that loves their home in the water and hates most to leave it, and he makes it jist as hard fur 'em as he kin. What the game fisher likes is the smallest kind of a hook, the thinnest line, and a fish that it takes a good while to weaken. The longer the weak'nin' business kin be spun out, the more the sport. The idee is to let the fish think there's a chance fur him to git away. That's jist like the cat with her mouse. She lets the little creetur hop off, but the minnit he gits fur enough away, she jumps on him and jabs him with her claws, and then, if there's any game left in him, she lets him try again. Of course the game fisher could have a strong line and a stout pole and git his fish in a good sight quicker, if he wanted to, but that wouldn't be sport. He couldn't give him the butt and spin him out, and reel him in, and let him jump and run till his pluck is clean worn out. Now, I likes to git my fish ashore with all the pluck in 'em. It makes 'em taste better. And as fur fun, I'll be bound I've had jist as much of that, and more, too, than most of these fellers who are so dreadful anxious to have everythin' jist right, and think they can't go fishin' till they've spent enough money to buy a suit of Sunday clothes. As a gen'ral rule they're a solemn lot, and work pretty hard at their fun. When I work I want to be paid fur it, and when I go in fur fun I want to take it easy and cheerful. Now I wouldn't say so much agen these fellers," said old Peter, as he arose and put his empty pipe on a little shelf under the porch-roof, "if it wasn't for one thing, and that is, that they think that their kind of fishin' is the only kind worth considerin'. The way they look down upon plain Christian fishin' is enough to rile a hitchin'-post. I don't want to say nothin' agen no man's way of attendin' to his own affairs, whether it's kitchen-gardenin', or whether it's fishin', if he says nothin' agen my way; but when he looks down on me, and grins at me, I want to haul myself up, and grin at him, if I kin. And in this case, I kin. I s'pose the house-cat and the cat-fisher (by which I don't mean the man who fishes for cat-fish) was both made as they is, and they can't help it; but that don't give 'em no right to put on airs before other bein's, who gits their meat with a square kill. Good-night. And sence I've talked so much about it, I've a mind to go fishin' with you to-morrow myself."

The next morning found old Peter of the same mind, and after breakfast he proceeded to fit me out for a day of what he called "plain Christian trout-fishin'." He gave me a reed rod, about nine feet long, light, strong, and nicely balanced. The tackle he produced was not of the fancy order, but his lines were of fine strong linen, and his hooks were of good shape, clean and sharp, and snooded to the lines with a neatness that indicated the hand of a man who had been where he learned to wear little gold rings in his ears.

"Here are some of these feather insects," he said, "which you kin take along if you like." And he handed me a paper containing a few artificial flies. "They're pretty nat'ral," he said, "and the hooks is good. A man who came here fishin' gave 'em to me, but I shan't want 'em to-day. At this time of year grasshoppers is the best bait in the kind of place where we're goin' to fish. The stream, after it comes down from the mountain, runs through half a mile of medder land before it strikes into the woods agen. A grasshopper is a little creetur that's got as much conceit as if his jinted legs was fish-poles, and he thinks he kin jump over this narrer run of water whenever he pleases; but he don't always do it, and then if he doesn't git snapped up by the trout that lie along the banks in the medder, he is floated along into the woods, where there's always fish enough to come to the second table."

Having got me ready, Peter took his own particular pole, which he assured me he had used for eleven years, and hooking on his left arm a good-sized basket, which his elder pretty daughter had packed with cold meat, bread, butter, and preserves, we started forth for a three-mile walk to the fishing-ground. The day was a favorable one for our purpose, the sky being sometimes over-clouded, which was good for fishing, and also for walking on a highroad; and sometimes bright, which was good for effects of mountain-scenery. Not far from the spot where old Peter proposed to begin our sport, a small frame-house stood by the roadside, and here the old man halted and entered the open door without knocking or giving so much as a premonitory stamp. I followed, imitating my companion in leaving my pole outside, which appeared to be the only ceremony that the etiquette of those parts required of visitors. In the room we entered, a small man in his shirt-sleeves sat mending a basket-handle. He nodded to Peter, and Peter nodded to him.

"We've come up a-fishin'," said the old man. "Kin your boys give us some grasshoppers?"

"I don't know that they've got any ready ketched," said he, "for I reckon I used what they had this mornin'. But they kin git you some. Here, Dan, you and Sile go and ketch Mr. Gruse and this young man some grasshoppers. Take that mustard-box, and see that you git it full."

Peter and I now took seats, and the conversation began about a black cow which Peter had to sell, and which the other was willing to buy if the old man would trade for sheep, which animals, however, the basket-mender did not appear just at that time to have in his possession. As I was not very much interested in this subject, I walked to the back-door and watched two small boys in scanty shirts and trousers, and ragged straw hats, who were darting about in the grass catching grasshoppers, of which insects, judging by the frequent pounces of the boys, there seemed a plentiful supply.

"Got it full?" said their father, when the boys came in.

"Crammed," said Dan.

Old Peter took the little can, pressed the top firmly on, put it in his coat-tail pocket, and rose to go. "You'd better think about that cow, Barney," said he. He said nothing to the boys about the box of bait; but I could not let them catch grasshoppers for us for nothing, and I took a dime from my pocket, and gave it to Dan. Dan grinned, and Sile looked sheepishly happy, and at the sight of the piece of silver an expression of interest came over the face of the father. "Wait a minute," said he, and he went into a little room that seemed to be a kitchen. Returning, he brought with him a small string of trout. "Do you want to buy some fish?" he said. "These is nice fresh ones. I ketched 'em this mornin'."

To offer to sell fish to a man who is just about to go out to catch them for himself might, in most cases, be considered an insult, but it was quite evident that nothing of the kind was intended by Barney. He probably thought that if I bought grasshoppers, I might buy fish. "You kin have 'em for a quarter," he said.

It was derogatory to my pride to buy fish at such a moment, but the man looked very poor, and there was a shade of anxiety on his face which touched me. Old Peter stood by without saying a word. "It might be well," I said, turning to him, "to buy these fish, for we may not catch enough for supper."

"Such things do happen," said the old man.

"Well," said I, "if we have these we shall feel safe in any case." And I took the fish and gave the man a quarter. It was not, perhaps, a professional act, but the trout were well worth the money, and I felt that I was doing a deed of charity.

Old Peter and I now took our rods, and crossed the road into an enclosed field, and thence into a wide stretch of grass land, bounded by hills in front of us and to the right, while a thick forest lay to the left. We had walked but a short distance, when Peter said: "I'll go down into the woods, and try my luck there, and you'd better go along up stream, about a quarter of a mile, to where it's rocky. P'raps you ain't used to fishin' in the woods, and you might git your line cotched. You'll find the trout'll bite in the rough water."

"Where is the stream?" I asked.

"This is it," he said, pointing to a little brook, which was scarcely too wide for me to step across, "and there's fish right here, but they're hard to ketch, fur they git plenty of good livin' and are mighty sassy about their eatin'. But you kin ketch 'em up there."

Old Peter now went down toward the woods, while I walked up the little stream. I had seen trout-brooks before, but never one so diminutive as this. However, when I came nearer to the point where the stream issued from between two of the foot-hills of the mountains, which lifted their forest-covered heights in the distance, I found it wider and shallower, breaking over its rocky bottom in sparkling little cascades.

Fishing in such a jolly little stream, surrounded by this mountain scenery, and with the privileges of the beautiful situation all to myself, would have been a joy to me if I had had never a bite. But no such ill-luck befell me. Peter had given me the can of grass-hoppers after putting half of them into his own bait-box, and these I used with much success. It was grasshopper season, and the trout were evidently on the lookout for them. I fished in the ripples under the little waterfalls; and every now and then I drew out a lively trout. Most of these were of moderate size, and some of them might have been called small. The large ones probably fancied the forest shades, where old Peter went. But all I caught were fit for the table, and I was very well satisfied with the result of my sport.

About noon I began to feel hungry, and thought it time to look up the old man, who had the lunch-basket. I walked down the bank of the brook, and some time before I reached the woods I came to a place where it expanded to a width of about ten feet. The water here was very clear, and the motion quiet, so that I could easily see to the bottom, which did not appear to be more than a foot below the surface. Gazing into this transparent water, as I walked, I saw a large trout glide across the stream, and disappear under the grassy bank which overhung the opposite side. I instantly stopped. This was a much larger fish than any I had caught, and I determined to try for him.

I stepped back from the bank, so as to be out of sight, and put a fine grasshopper on my hook; then I lay, face downward, on the grass, and worked myself slowly forward until I could see the middle of the stream; then quietly raising my pole, I gave my grasshopper a good swing, as if he had made a wager to jump over the stream at its widest part. But as he certainly would have failed in such an ambitious endeavor, especially if he had been caught by a puff of wind, I let him come down upon the surface of the water, a little beyond the middle of the brook. Grasshoppers do not sink when they fall into the water, and so I kept this fellow upon the surface, and gently moved him along, as if, with all the conceit taken out of him by the result of his ill-considered leap, he was ignominiously endeavoring to swim to shore. As I did this, I saw the trout come out from under the bank, move slowly toward the grasshopper, and stop directly under him. Trembling with anxiety and eager expectation, I endeavored to make the movements of the insect still more natural, and, as far as I was able, I threw into him a sudden perception of his danger, and a frenzied desire to get away. But, either the trout had had all the grasshoppers he wanted, or he was able, from long experience, to perceive the difference between a natural exhibition of emotion and a histrionic imitation of it, for he slowly turned, and, with a few slight movements of his tail, glided back under the bank. In vain did the grasshopper continue his frantic efforts to reach the shore; in vain did he occasionally become exhausted, and sink a short distance below the surface; in vain did he do everything that he knew, to show that he appreciated what a juicy and delicious morsel he was, and how he feared that the trout might yet be tempted to seize him; the fish did not come out again.

Then I withdrew my line, and moved back from the stream. I now determined to try Mr. Trout with a fly, and I took out the paper old Peter Gruse had given me. I did not know exactly what kind of winged insects were in order at this time of the year, but I was sure that yellow butterflies were not particular about just what month it was, so long as the sun shone warmly. I therefore chose that one of Peter's flies which was made of the yellowest feathers, and, removing the snood and hook from my line, I hastily attached this fly, which was provided with a hook quite suitable for my desired prize. Crouching on the grass, I again approached the brook. Gaily flitting above the glassy surface of the water, in all the fancied security of tender youth and innocence, came my yellow fly. Backward and forward over the water he gracefully flew, sometimes rising a little into the air, as if to view the varied scenery of the woods and mountains, and then settling for a moment close to the surface, to better inspect his glittering image as it came up from below, and showing in his every movement his intense enjoyment of summer-time and life.

Out from his dark retreat now came the trout, and settling quietly at the bottom of the brook, he appeared to regard the venturesome insect with a certain interest. But he must have detected the iron-barb of vice beneath the mask of blitheful innocence, for, after a short deliberation, the trout turned and disappeared under the bank. As he slowly moved away, he seemed to be bigger than ever. I must catch that fish! Surely he would bite at something. It was quite evident that his mind was not wholly unsusceptible to emotions emanating from an awakening appetite, and I believed that if he saw exactly what he wanted, he would not neglect an opportunity of availing himself of it. But what did he want? I must certainly find out. Drawing myself back again, I took off the yellow fly, and put on another. This was a white one, with black blotches, like a big miller moth which had fallen into an ink-pot. It was surely a conspicuous creature, and as I crept forward and sent it swooping over the stream, I could not see how any trout, with a single insectivorous tooth in his head, could fail to rise to such an occasion. But this trout did not rise. He would not even come out from under his bank to look at the swiftly flitting creature. He probably could see it well enough from where he was.

But I was not to be discouraged. I put on another fly; a green one with a red tail. It did not look like any insect that I had ever seen, but I thought that the trout might know more about such things than I. He did come out to look at it, but probably considering it a product of that modern æstheticism which sacrifices natural beauty to mediæval crudeness of color and form, he retired without evincing any disposition to countenance this style of art.

It was evident that it would be useless to put on any other flies, for the two I had left were a good deal bedraggled, and not nearly so attractive as those I had used. Just before leaving the house that morning, Peter's son had given me a wooden match-box filled with worms for bait, which, although I did not expect to need, I put in my pocket. As a last resort I determined to try the trout with a worm. I selected the plumpest and most comely of the lot; I put a new hook on my line; I looped him about it in graceful coils, and cautiously approached the water, as before. Now a worm never attempts to wildly leap across a flowing brook, nor does he flit in thoughtless innocence through the sunny air, and over the bright transparent stream. If he happens to fall into the water, he sinks to the bottom; and if he be of a kind not subject to drowning, he generally endeavors to secrete himself under a stone, or to burrow in the soft mud. With this knowledge of his nature I gently dropped my worm upon the surface of the stream, and then allowed him slowly to sink. Out sailed the trout from under the bank, but stopped before reaching the sinking worm. There was a certain something in his action which seemed to indicate a disgust at the sight of such plebeian food, and a fear seized me that he might now swim off, and pay no further attention to my varied baits. Suddenly there was a ripple in the water, and I felt a pull on the line. Instantly I struck; and then there was a tug. My blood boiled through every vein and artery, and I sprang to my feet. I did not give him the butt; I did not let him run with yards of line down the brook; nor reel him in, and let him make another mad course up stream; I did not turn him over as he jumped into the air; nor endeavor, in any way, to show him that I understood those tricks, which his depraved nature prompted him to play upon the angler. With an absolute dependence upon the strength of old Peter's tackle, I lifted the fish. Out he came from the water, which held him with a gentle suction as if unwilling to let him go, and then he whirled through the air like a meteor flecked with rosy fire, and landed on the fresh green grass a dozen feet behind me. Down on my knees I dropped before him as he tossed and rolled, his beautiful spots and colors glistening in the sun. He was truly a splendid trout, fully a foot long, round and heavy. Carefully seizing him, I easily removed the hook from the bony roof of his capacious mouth thickly set with sparkling teeth, and then I tenderly killed him, with all his pluck, as old Peter would have said, still in him.

I covered the rest of the fish in my basket with wet plantain leaves, and laid my trout king on this cool green bed. Then I hurried off to the old man, whom I saw coming out of the woods. When I opened my basket and showed him what I had caught, Peter looked surprised, and, taking up the trout, examined it.

"Why, this is a big fellow," he said. "At first I thought it was Barney Sloat's boss trout, but it isn't long enough for him. Barney showed me his trout, that gen'rally keeps in a deep pool, where a tree has fallen over the stream down there. Barney tells me he often sees him, and he's been tryin' fur two years to ketch him, but he never has, and I say he never will, fur them big trout's got too much sense to fool round any kind of victuals that's got a string to it. They let a little fish eat all he wants, and then they eat him. How did you ketch this one?"

I gave an account of the manner of the capture, to which Peter listened with interest and approval.

"If you'd a stood off and made a cast at that feller, you'd either have caught him at the first flip, which isn't likely, as he didn't seem to want no feather flies, or else you'd a skeered him away. That's all well enough in the tumblin' water, where you gen'rally go fur trout, but the man that's got the true feelin' fur fish will try to suit his idees to theirs, and if he keeps on doin' that, he's like to learn a thing or two that may do him good. That's a fine fish, and you ketched him well. I've got a lot of 'em, but nothin' of that heft."

After luncheon we fished for an hour or two with no result worth recording, and then we started for home. A couple of partridges ran across the road some distance ahead of us, and these gave Peter an idea.

"Do you know," said he, "if things go on as they're goin' on now, that there'll come a time when it won't be considered high-toned sport to shoot a bird slam-bang dead. The game gunners will pop 'em with little harpoons, with long threads tied to 'em, and the feller that can tire out his bird, and haul him in with the longest and thinnest piece of spool thread, will be the crackest sportsman."

At this point I remarked to my companion that perhaps he was a little hard on the game fishermen.

"Well," said old Peter, with a smile on his corrugated visage, "I reckon I'd have to do a lot of talkin' before I'd git even with 'em, fur the way they give me the butt for my style of fishin'. What I say behind their backs I say to their faces. I seed one of these fellers once with a fish on his hook, that he was runnin' up an' down the stream like a chased chicken. 'Why don't you pull him in?' says I. 'And break my rod an' line?' says he. 'Why don't you have a stronger line and pole?' says I. 'There wouldn't be no science in that,' says he. 'If it's your science you want to show off,' says I, 'you ought to fish for mud eels. There's more game in 'em than there is in any other fish round here, and as they're mighty lively out of water you might play one of 'em fur half an hour after you got him on shore, and it would take all your science to keep him from reelin' up his end of the line faster than you could yourn.'"

When we reached the farm the old man went into the barn, and I took the fish into the house. I found the two pretty daughters in the large room, where the eating and some of the cooking was done. I opened my basket, and with great pride showed them the big trout I had caught. They evidently thought it was a large fish, but they looked at each other, and smiled in a way that I did not understand. I had expected from them, at least, as much admiration for my prize and my skill as their father had shown.

"You don't seem to think much of this fine trout that I took such trouble to catch," I remarked.

"You mean," said the elder girl, with a laugh, "that you bought of Barney Sloat."

I looked at her in astonishment.

"Barney was along here to-day," she said, "and he told about your buying your fish of him."

"Bought of him!" I exclaimed, indignantly. "A little string of fish at the bottom of the basket I bought of him, but all the others, and this big one, I caught myself."

"Oh, of course," said the pretty daughter, "bought the little ones and caught all the big ones!"

"Barney Sloat ought to have kept his mouth shut," said the younger pretty daughter, looking at me with an expression of pity. "He'd got his money, and he hadn't no business to go telling on people. Nobody likes that sort of thing. But this big fish is a real nice one, and you shall have it for your supper."

"Thank you," I said, with dignity, and left the room.

I did not intend to have any further words with these young women on this subject, but I cannot deny that I was annoyed and mortified. This was the result of a charitable action. I think I was never more proud of anything than of catching that trout; and it was a good deal of a downfall to suddenly find myself re-garded as a mere city man fishing with a silver hook. But, after all, what did it matter?

The boy who did not seem to be accounted a member of the family came into the house, and as he passed me he smiled good-humoredly, and said: "Buyed 'em!"

I felt like throwing a chair at him, but refrained out of respect to my host. Before supper the old man came out on to the porch where I was sitting. "It seems," said he, "that my gals has got it inter their heads that you bought that big fish of Barney Sloat, and as I can't say I seed you ketch it, they're not willin' to give in, 'specially as I didn't git no such big one. 'Tain't wise to buy fish when you're goin' fishin' yourself. It's pretty certain to tell agen you."

"You ought to have given me that advice before," I said, somewhat shortly. "You saw me buy the fish."

"You don't s'pose," said old Peter, "that I'm goin' to say anythin' to keep money out of my neighbor's pockets. We don't do that way in these parts. But I've told the gals they're not to speak another word about it, so you needn't give your mind no worry on that score. And now let's go in to supper. If you're as hungry as I am, there won't be many of them fish left fur breakfast."

That evening, as we were sitting smoking on the porch, old Peter's mind reverted to the subject of the unfounded charge against me. "It goes pretty hard," he remarked, "to have to stand up and take a thing you don' like when there's no call fur it. It's bad enough when there is a call fur it. That matter about your fish buyin' reminds me of what happened two summers ago to my sister, or ruther to her two little boys—or, more correct yit, to one of 'em. Them was two cur'ous little boys. They was allus tradin' with each other. Their father deals mostly in horses, and they must have got it from him. At the time I'm tellin' of they'd traded everythin' they had, and when they hadn't nothin' else left to swap they traded names. Joe he took Johnny's name, and Johnny he took Joe's. Jist about when they'd done this, they both got sick with sumthin' or other, the oldest one pretty bad, the other not much. Now there ain't no doctor inside of twenty miles of where my sister lives. But there's one who sometimes has a call to go through that part of the country, and the people about there is allus very glad when they chance to be sick when he comes along. Now this good luck happened to my sister, fur the doctor come by jist at this time. He looks into the state of the boys, and while their mother has gone downstairs he mixes some medicine he has along with him. 'What's your name?' he says to the oldest boy when he'd done it. Now as he'd traded names with his brother, fair and square, he wasn't goin' back on the trade, and he said, 'Joe.' 'And my name's Johnny,' up and says the other one. Then the doctor he goes and gives the bottle of medicine to their mother, and says he: 'This medicine is fur Joe. You must give him a tablespoonful every two hours. Keep up the treatment, and he'll be all right. As fur Johnny, there's nothin' much the matter with him. He don't need no medicine.' And then he went away. Every two hours after that Joe, who wasn't sick worth mentionin', had to swallow a dose of horrid stuff, and pretty soon he took to his bed, and Johnny he jist played round and got well in the nat'ral way. Joe's mother kept up the treatment, gittin' up in the night to feed that stuff to him; but the poor little boy got wuss and wuss, and one mornin' he says to his mother, says he: 'Mother, I guess I'm goin' to die, and I'd ruther do that than take any more of that medicine, and I wish you'd call Johnny and we'll trade names back agen, and if he don't want to come and do it, you kin tell him he kin keep the old minkskin I gave him to boot, on account of his name havin' a Wesley in it.' 'Trade names,' says his mother, 'what do you mean by that?' And then he told her what he and Johnny had done. 'And did you ever tell anybody about this?' says she. 'Nobody but Dr. Barnes,' says he. 'After that I got sick and forgot it.' When my sister heard that, an idee struck into her like you put a fork into an apple dumplin'. Traded names, and told the doctor! She'd all along thought it strange that the boy that seemed wuss should be turned out, and the other one put under treatment; but it wasn't fur her to set up her opinion agen that of a man like Dr. Barnes. Down she went, in about seventeen jumps, to where Eli Timmins, the hired man, was ploughin' in the corn. 'Take that horse out of that,' she hollers, 'and you may kill him if you have to, but git Dr. Barnes here before my little boy dies.' When the doctor come he heard the story, and looked at the sick youngster, and then says he: 'If he'd kept his minkskin, and not hankered after a Wesley to his name, he'd a had a better time of it. Stop the treatment, and he'll be all right.' Which she did; and he was. Now it seems to me that this is a good deal like your case. You've had to take a lot of medicine that didn't belong to you, and I guess it's made you feel pretty bad; but I've told my gals to stop the treatment, and you'll be all right in the mornin'. Good-night. Your candlestick is on the kitchen table."

For two days longer I remained in this neighborhood, wandering alone over the hills, and up the mountain-sides, and by the brooks, which tumbled and gurgled through the lonely forest. Each evening I brought home a goodly supply of trout, but never a great one like the noble fellow for which I angled in the meadow stream.

On the morning of my departure I stood on the porch with old Peter waiting for the arrival of the mail driver, who was to take me to the nearest railroad town.

"I don't want to say nothin'," remarked the old man, "that would keep them fellers with the jinted poles from stoppin' at my house when they comes to these parts a-fishin'. I ain't got no objections to their poles; 'tain't that. And I don't mind nuther their standin' off, and throwin' their flies as fur as they've a mind to; that's not it. And it ain't even the way they have of worryin' their fish. I wouldn't do it myself, but if they like it, that's their business. But what does rile me is the cheeky way in which they stand up and say that there isn't no decent way of fishin' but their way. And that to a man that's ketched more fish, of more different kinds, with more game in 'em, and had more fun at it, with a lot less money, and less tomfoolin' than any fishin' feller that ever come here and talked to me like an old cat tryin' to teach a dog to ketch rabbits. No, sir; agen I say that I don't take no money fur entertainin' the only man that ever come out here to go a-fishin' in a plain, Christian way. But if you feel tetchy about not payin' nothin', you kin send me one of them poles in three pieces, a good strong one, that'll lift Barney Sloat's trout, if ever I hook him."

I sent him the rod; and next summer I am going out to see him use it.

www.ingramcontent.com/pod-product-compliance
Lightning Source LLC
Chambersburg PA
CBHW050912120626
46552CB00004B/1542